P9-DGV-737

0000183715283

Also by
JAMES MARSHALL
George and Martha
What's the Matter with Carruthers?
Yummers!

For Adolph, Adrienne,
Ronald, and Philip

Library of Congress Cataloging in Publication Data

Marshall, James, 1942-
   George and Martha encore.

   SUMMARY: In five brief episodes two hippopotamuses
reinforce their friendship.
   [1. Friendship--Fiction] I. Title.
PZ10.3.M3535Gg   [E]   73-5845
ISBN 0-395-17512-7

COPYRIGHT © 1973 BY JAMES MARSHALL

All rights reserved. For information about permission
to reproduce selections from this book, write to
Permissions, Houghton Mifflin Company, 215 Park Avenue
South, New York, New York 10003.

PRINTED IN CHINA

ISBN: 0-395-17512-7 REINFORCED EDITION

ISBN: 0-395-25379-9 SANDPIPER PAPERBOUND EDITION

SCP   40 39 38 37 36 35
4500529993

George and Martha were having a disagreement.

"I think dancing is dumb," said George.

"Dancing is not dumb!" exclaimed Martha.

"Dancing is fun! And if you don't come to my dance recital, I'll be very angry!"

So, of course, George went to Martha's recital.

"I'm going to hate this," he said to himself.

But what a surprise for George!

Martha's Dance of the Happy Butterfly

was so impressive.

"Dancing looks like fun," said George.

The next day George went to dancing class.

"You see," said Martha, "dancing is fun!"

Very soon George was in his own dance recital.

Martha said that his Mexican Hat Dance was

the best she had ever seen.

George went to Martha's house for his French lesson.

"Bonjour, Martha," said George.

"Bonjour, George," said Martha.

George sat next to Martha on the sofa.

"How do you say 'Give me a kiss' in French?" asked George.

"You say 'Voulez-vous m'embrasser?'"* answered Martha.

And that is just what George did.

"Tee-hee," said Martha.

"I knew you were going to do that."

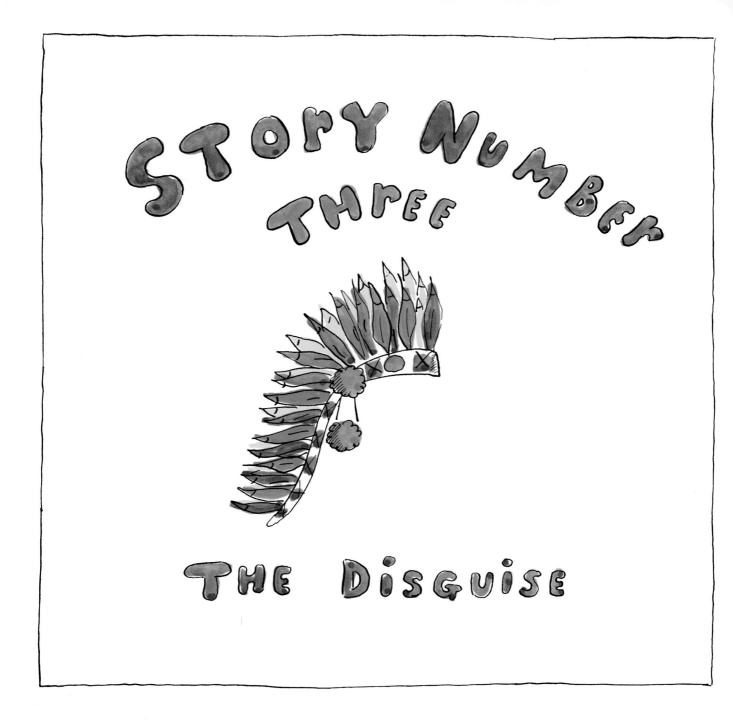

STORY NUMBER THREE

THE DISGUISE

George decided to dress up as an Indian.

"This disguise will really fool Martha," he chuckled.

"She'll never recognize me."

But Martha wasn't fooled a bit.

"Hi, George," she said.

"Why are you wearing that Indian costume?"

George was so disappointed.

He walked away hanging his head.

Martha felt simply awful.

She hadn't meant to hurt George's feelings.

"George," said Martha. "I would never have recognized you if it hadn't been for your bright smiling eyes. It's so hard to disguise smiling eyes."

And, of course, George felt much, much better.

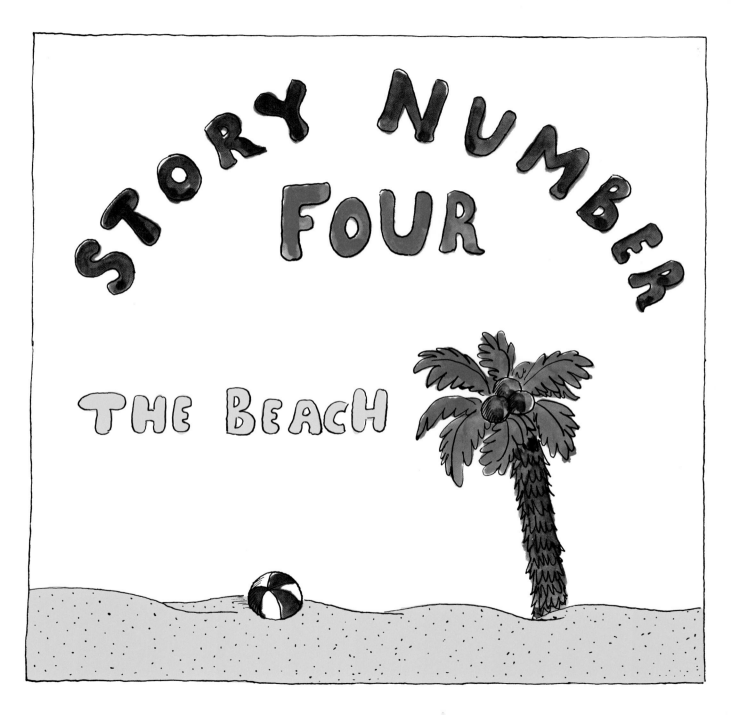

One day George and Martha went to the beach.

"I love the beach!" exclaimed Martha.

"So do I," said George.

"However, we must be sure to put on our suntan lotion."

But Martha refused to put on her suntan lotion.

"You'll be sorry," George called out.

"Oh, pooh," said his friend.

"You're a fuss-budget, George."

Martha was having such a lovely time.

The next day Martha had a terrible sunburn!

She felt all hot and itchy.

But George never said "I told you so."

Because that's not what friends are for.

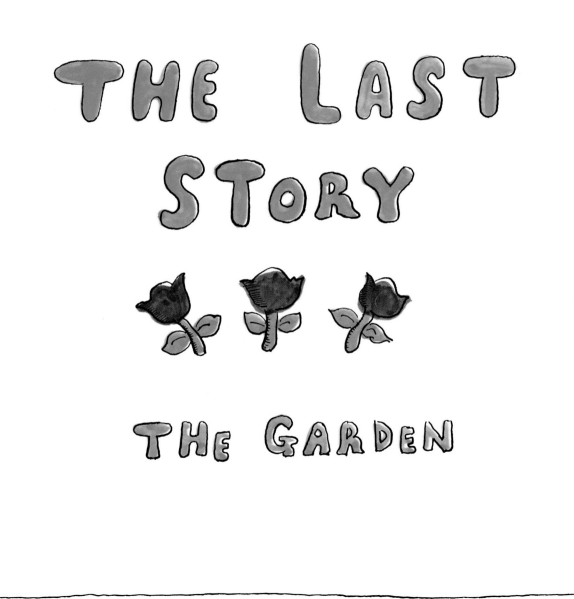

THE LAST STORY

THE GARDEN

Martha was so discouraged.

Her garden was an ugly mess of weeds.

"I just don't seem to have a green thumb," she sobbed.

George hated to see Martha unhappy.

He wanted so much to help.

Suddenly George had a splendid idea.

He went to the florist and bought

all the tulips in the shop.

Tulips were Martha's favorite flowers.

Very quietly George crept into Martha's garden

and stuck the tulips in the ground.

But just then Martha happened to look out the window.

"Oh, dear," said George.

"You're always catching me."

But Martha was so pleased.

"Dear George," she said.

"I would much rather have a friend like you

than all the gardens in the world."